For Lynn,
My fellow Heat scorer.

Yours,
s[...]

Hee
Hee
Hee...

Pedigree Girls

Pedigree Girls

Sherwin Tjia

INSOMNIAC PRESS

Edited by Richard Almonte
Copy-edited by Jan Barbieri
Designed by Sherwin Tjia

National Library of Canada Cataloguing in Publication Data

Tjia, Sherwin, 1975–
    Pedigree girls

Includes index.
ISBN 1-895837-10-3

I. Title.

PN6734.P42T54 2001   741.5'971   C2001-930388-2

The publisher gratefully acknowledges the support of the Canada Council, the Ontario Arts Council and Department of Canadian Heritage through the Book Publishing Industry Development Program.

Printed and bound in Canada.

Insomniac Press, 192 Spadina Avenue, Suite 403,
Toronto, Ontario, Canada, M5T 2C2
www.insomniacpress.com

**For the Queen
Vas Deum**

*"And I could live on cold desire,
on the remnants of your fire,
like one who knows
who just believes—
that this is all some joke
and the punchline's peace,
Lord have mercy, have compassion,
You take absolute action."*

**—Ryan Kamstra,
from "God"**

PEDIGREE GIRLS

PEDIGREE GIRLS

PEDIGREE GIRLS

PEDIGREE GIRLS

The other day I laughed so hard I almost sneezed my tampon out.

Does that happen a lot?

If I'm lucky.

PEDIGREE GIRLS

Wanna date me?

No.

Wanna date me?

No.

Wanna date me?

And they say the art of conversation is dead.

PEDIGREE GIRLS

I hate my thighs.

Me too.

You hate your thighs too?

No, I hate *your* thighs.

Bitch.

Skank.

PEDIGREE GIRLS

PEDIGREE GIRLS

PEDIGREE GIRLS

PEDIGREE GIRLS

PEDIGREE GIRLS

PEDIGREE GIRLS

PEDIGREE GIRLS

I need a new skirt. — Good *luck.*

What's *that* supposed to mean? — Nothing.

Okay. Yeah. Sure. Whatever. — Okay. Yeah. Sure. *Whatever.*

PEDIGREE GIRLS

I didn't know your father was a diplomat. — Oh. Yeah. He is.

Must be nice. Seeing other countries, diplomatic immunity, cushy summer jobs, plush hotels, fancy dinners... — Your point?

I heard on the news this morning that your sister was kidnapped and is being held for ransom. — *Dammit!* Not *again!*

PEDIGREE GIRLS

Did you see Carrie Hunt? — You mean, Hairy Cunt?

Yeah, she's lost like 50 pounds! — Must've gone to fat camp.

No. She wasn't there. — *I don't!* — How do *you* know that?

PEDIGREE GILRS

PEDIGREE GIRLS

PEDIGREE GIRLS

PEDIGREE GIRLS

In french, they say, "Faire la leche vitrine".

Yeah, "window licking".

I want that Prada dress so bad.

I went in there the other day.

Did you try it on? How did it feel?

Like I can't afford it.

PEDIGREE GIRLS

I'm sooo hungry.

And I want a guy.

I'm sick of your incessant horny complaints and unwillingness to do anything about it!

And I'm sick of your body-image-issue, eating disor-der bullshit!

Satisfied?

Rarely.

PEDIGREE GIRLS

Know Tara?

Yeah.

Her posse's going to change her image.

They've got to *find* it first.

PEDIGREE GIRLS

Who's the new girl?

Andrea Cook.

Should we know her?

Not ugly enough to ignore. Not pretty enough to hate... Sure.

How do you *do* that?

Just talented, I guess.

PEDIGREE GIRLS

My dad pays more attention to me than he does to my mom.

That's fucked.

My mom's like scenery. In fact, he's taking *me* out to dinner tonight!

Wow!

Christ, what should I do?

Well, your dad *is* pretty hot...

PEDIGREE GIRLS

So, are you going to stay with that haircut or what?

I don't know. I keep changing my mind.

You should come with me and Mich. We'll introduce you to Matt. He'll take care of you. He's giving us all, like, a hip "fuck you" sort of cut.

I'm sooo jealous. You guys are, like, moving in a *direction* with your hair.

PEDIGREE GIRLS

I can make things move with my mind.

Prove it. Rub my nipples.

Feel it?

That's your *hand.*

Should I stop?

I didn't say that.

PEDIGREE GIRLS

So, my dad's finally dead. Cancer.

Oh, Ally. I'm sooo sorry. He used to teach me tennis.

I'm not sorry. Bastard used to beat up my mom every chance he got.

So that's what he meant.

About what?

When he said he was going home to practise his backhand.

PEDIGREE GIRLS

For fuck's sake, I can't believe they carded me at the door.

I mean, do I *look* younger than 18?

No. But you're acting like it.

PEDIGREE GIRLS

My entire family was shot to death last night during a botched robbery.

Omigod! Meaghan!

The house is sooo empty right now.

Listen, if there's anything I can do...

Well, actually, could you stop by the market and get some dip?

Awright! *Par-tay!*

PEDIGREE GIRLS

Those cheerleaders make me sick.

You're just jealous.

Only if I'm jealous of an STD-ridden *skank.*

She does have good hair.

Under her *arms.*

That's what I like about you. You're so friendly.

PEDIGREE GIRLS

You know, I feel weird about this. This is the last time we have sex. Never again!

See you next week?

Okay.

PEDIGREE GIRLS

My parents are going away for the weekend. Dad's finally got time off from his firm and Mom has sick days coming.

They've left their cellphones at home. They've got no one but each other to talk to for three whole days!

Uh-oh. That's grounds for divorce.

PEDIGREE GIRLS

Do you scream when you orgasm?

Just a little.

Like how?

Like... um... *ooooohh.*

Now, don't be shy.

Okay, we're *done* here.

PEDIGREE GIRLS

Mom was drunk and we ran into a tree last night.

Omigod! Are you okay?

Yeah. We've got one of those sports utility vehicles.

Oh good! Those are like a gated community on wheels.

PEDIGREE GIRLS

PEDIGREE GIRLS

PEDIGREE GIRLS

PEDIGREE GIRLS

I need a nose job.

No you don't.

Yes I *do*. It's huge. It's bulbous. It feels to me like that thing on the front of a train. A cowcatcher, or whatever it's called.

Amy, you're so full of shit it's not funny.

So you'll lend me the money?

PEDIGREE GIRLS

My parents don't want me to have sex until I'm 18.

Wow. That's pretty rigid.

Next they'll want me to stop snorting coke.

PEDIGREE GIRLS

Boy, Steph and Jenn sure became friends fast.

Yeah. I mean, they're so mismatched. What are they doing together?

Like, what *aren't* they doing together?

PEDIGREE GIRLS

Trust Gail to put on her knee-high fuck-me boots right after school lets out.

She's such a slut.

That's why they call her "Head Girl", I guess.

PEDIGREE GIRLS

I've thought long and hard all winter about what I want to accomplish this summer.

Shopping?

And plenty of it.

PEDIGREE GIRLS

Dairy Queen?   Umm...

Yes or no!   Um, okay!

In this business, you're either on your way, or *in the way.*

PEDIGREE GIRLS

PEDIGREE GIRLS

PEDIGREE GIRLS

PEDIGREE GIRLS

Jason just dumped me.

Oh Kelly, you must feel *terrible!*

I swear... you're *psychic!*

PEDIGREE GIRLS

God, Edie, you're sooo beautiful.

Oh, stop.

Don't stop.

PEDIGREE GIRLS

My dad's hitting my mom. What should I do?

Kill him.

Ann Landers, eat your heart out.

PEDIGREE GIRLS

God, I see her face every-where. I'm just so sick of hearing about her. I mean, she's all anyone's talking about.

Everyone gets their 15 minutes of fame, sure. But this is getting *ridiculous.*

It's *such* a popularity contest. Missing girls get all the luck.

PEDIGREE GIRLS

See the posters?

That missing girl?

Not very pretty.

Nope. Nothing to write home about.

I mean, why would *anyone* kidnap *her?*

Really, it's for the best.

PEDIGREE GIRLS

So, all the posters of missing white kids were really nicely laid out, in colour, and on nice paper...

...while all the posters of minority kids were in blurry black and white, poorly designed, and on that dull recycled stuff.

Those wacky Alabama cops!

PEDIGREE GIRLS

The models are getting skinnier!

Well, of course.

Nobody ever got rich by making people feel *good* about themselves.

Except Oprah.

We have Oprah to thank.

PEDIGREE GIRLS

Get a load of this: "Blonde is Back!", "Blonde Ambition", "The New Blonde".

Are you reading *Vogue*? *Harper's Bazaar*?

Nope.

Mein Kampf.

PEDIGREE GIRLS

My dad's company just downsized 900 workers. He wanted to cut the fat, streamline things. Soo much more efficient, I think.

You're so right. It occurred to me the other day that I could save time and energy by pissing in the shower.

Our *dorm* shower?!

Efficiency's not *everything*, Linds.

PEDIGREE GIRLS

I've got a pimple on my left butt-cheek. I never thought pimples grew there, but they *do*. Whenever I sit down, I...

...get right back up again. My boyfriend tried to pop it with a pin the other night, but it didn't work.

Abby? Like, **too much information!**

PEDIGREE GIRLS

Watch this... *You fat cow! You're stupid and ugly, and you'll never get a date!*

Well fuck you too!

There's nothing really *wrong* with her, is there?   No.

PEDIGREE GIRLS

Now don't get me wrong...

...it's not that I don't like rules...

...I just hate having them apply to me.

PEDIGREE GIRLS

Yeah, I was in ballet until I was 17 and in gymnastics until I was 16...

...and I used to put my ankles behind my neck when David and I had sex.

All I ask is that you use your powers for good instead of evil.

PEDIGREE GIRLS

Come to my birthday.

Okay. What should I wear?

Come naked.

What?!

We're going to eat you.

PEDIGREE GIRLS

It's important to *know* we're privileged.

Why?

So we can enjoy it *more*.

PEDIGREE GILRS

PEDIGREE GILRS

PEDIGREE GILRS

PEDIGREE GIRLS

PEDIGREE GIRLS

PEDIGREE GIRLS

PEDIGREE GIRLS

So, he came into the room, gave me flowers, poured me a drink, and then he kissed me.

Awww. How romantic!

It would've been even more romantic if I was allowed to go *home!*

PEDIGREE GIRLS

So, we tormented this girl mercilessly! We wouldn't let up.

Yeah?

And you know what she goes and does? She *hangs* herself!

Oh my God!

What a *loser.*

PEDIGREE GIRLS

What about him?

He's cute. But he's black.

So what? He's sooo hot.

Maeve, you're the one who likes black guys.

So you'd never date one?

Maybe just to piss off my dad.

PEDIGREE GIRLS

How was the drive back from Montréal? Did it snow all the way back?

Um... I wasn't quite in control, but, you know, in a really *good* way.

One day I'm going to have to testify against you, aren't I?

PEDIGREE GIRLS

Whose breasts are these?

Hey!

Oh, I'm sorry. Am I making you uncomfortable?

PEDIGREE GIRLS

So, the other night, my girlfriend had taken downers and sleeping pills just before she came to my room. Her plan was to, like, die, and have me wake up to find her dead in the dorm, beside me.

Oh my God!

That is sooo clev— I mean, that's *really* bad!

PEDIGREE GIRLS

PEDIGREE GIRLS

PEDIGREE GIRLS

PEDIGREE GIRLS

You like
him?

Nah. Just
window
shopping.

PEDIGREE GIRLS

So what did Ms.
Webb have to
say to you?

She wanted to
know if I was
sorry.

I told her that ever since I
got to this school I haven't
been anything *but* sorry!

PEDIGREE GIRLS

Hooking.   Scoring.

Slapshots.

Who says
hockey's boring?

PEDIGREE GIRLS

My life was perfect until *you* showed up.

Like, why did you *fuck* with it?

PEDIGREE GIRLS

So, I rolled my kilt up another 3 inches and stuffed my bra. I had all the UCC boys drooling.

And, on top of that, I lined my lips in Vamp and wore that garter belt I got from my ex last Christmas.

Everything I do, I do for love.

PEDIGREE GIRLS

So, how come you tormented me so much in junior high?

I mean, your posse held me down on the ground while you *pissed* on my face. How could you *do* that to me?

It wasn't personal, you understand.

PEDIGREE GIRLS

God, I'm sleepy. I could use a coffee.

Or I could slap you.

PEDIGREE GIRLS

Alicia's drinking like a fish!

This morning she had three tequila shots before first period English. She was spouting crazy answers to every question!

You say that as if it were a *bad* thing.

PEDIGREE GIRLS

Kate, your dad tried to rape me last night.

He's under a lot of *pressure* these days. He's in the middle of a merger. It's a *billion-dollar* corporate takeover!

Where would he find the *time* to rape you?

PEDIGREE GIRLS

I hate school.

Me too.

You know, we should hit the road! Like Thelma and Louise! Go shoot up sexist truckers and stuff.

Yeah, but, like, not *die* or anything at the end.

PEDIGREE GIRLS

My brother likes you.

Oh yeah?

Yeah. He and his St. Andrew's buddies think you're hot.

Really?

No.

PEDIGREE GIRLS

Do you remember "Lost in Your Eyes" by Debbie Gibson?

Yeah. Whatever happened to her?

She changed her name to *Deborah* Gibson.

Oh, *Deborah* Gibson.

That's not better, is it?

PEDIGREE GIRLS

So I'm having this slumber party... Yeah?

All the coolest people will be there... And?

And?

PEDIGREE GIRLS

Don't forget your sexy lingerie for my slumber party. I don't have any.

That's too bad. My dad'll be disappointed. **What?!** Your *father*'ll be there?

Didn't I tell you? Must've slipped my mind.

PEDIGREE GIRLS

I'm not sure I'm comfortable with your *dad* being at your slumber party.

If you don't like it, don't come. Wait, that's *not* what I meant.

Stay a virgin, see if I care.

PEDIGREE GIRLS

Burp!

Excuse me.

Or don't. I don't give a shit.

PEDIGREE GIRLS

Have you had an AIDS test yet?

No. Why? Should I? Did you give it to me?

I didn't think I had it in me.

PEDIGREE GIRLS

So, Lucy says to him, "I'll hold the football, you run up and kick it."

So, Charlie Brown gets a running start, and at the last possible second, she pulls the ball away and he goes flying!

Ha-ha!

Wow. What a *cocktease*.

You said it.

PEDIGREE GIRLS

Geez, Kristy. Why did you *uninvite* Naomi to your party in front of the whole school?

Beacuse I wanted to.

Because it felt good.

PEDIGREE GIRLS

OW! I've got these sharp pains in my gut. I think I'm gonna pass out!

Be calm. Let me assess the situation first, before we do anything.

Hurry! It's getting worse. Oh, *fuck!*

I'll need to organize an inquiry.

Help!

PEDIGREE GIRLS

You're sooo lucky! Your brother is sooo nice! He takes you out to parties, he lends you his car...

My brother's an asshole. How come your brother's so good to you?

Well, I'm fucking him.

PEDIGREE GIRLS

God, Mare, you've got so much and I have so little.

I'd *love* to borrow that blue velvet skirt of yours when we all go to Jason's party.

Toucha my stuff, I breaka yo face.

PEDIGREE GIRLS

Listen, you can't go around treating people like shit. Your callous disregard for other people's feelings and desires contributes to an already toxic environment that...

...degrades those least equipped to help themselves, and exploits people's pain for a temporary psychological high.

What's your point?

PEDIGREE GIRLS

Where are all the boys?

This is an *all-girls* school.

Holy shit! Really?

Sorry to break it to you.

That's okay. Hey, listen, do you know how to use a strap-on?

PEDIGREE GIRLS

PEDIGREE GIRLS

PEDIGREE GIRLS

PEDIGREE GIRLS

I don't think we should be roomies anymore.

Why's that?

You don't leave money lying around like you used to.

PEDIGREE GIRLS

Sandra, I saw you cutting yourself again last night...

...and I think you should stop!

Imagine how *terrible* those scars will look with a sleeveless shirt.

PEDIGREE GIRLS

You saw Hillary cutting herself and didn't say anything? Why didn't you stop her?

If I had known she was a self-abuser I would have said something...

...but as it was, I thought she was slitting her wrists.

PEDIGREE GIRLS

So, what did he say?

He said that if he and I had sex I was consenting to having my like-ness, name and voice...

...exploited in any and all forms of media without compensation throughout the world and in perpetuity.

And you said?

What a bargain!

PEDIGREE GIRLS

So, how was Friday night?

We had sex.

Was it good? Were you impressed?

It was so bad, I should have pressed charges.

PEDIGREE GIRLS

Jess, don't hate me because I'm rich, thin, well-connected and beautiful, and you're none of the above.

I don't.

I hate you because you're conceited and **mean.**

PEDIGREE GIRLS

Whatever in the world are "cockles"?

Shackles for cocks?

You're a credit to your school, you know that?

PEDIGREE GIRLS

I am pretty.

I am going to make him *sit up*.

I can feel it coming on now.

You've been reading *Seventeen* again, haven't you?

PEDIGREE GIRLS

I can't believe you went on a date with Dylan. Sure, he's hot. Sure, sex with him would likely be a mind-blowing trip, singularly one of the most beautiful events of your life up till now.

But you're so smart. Intellectually, you're *heads and shoulders* above him.

I have my blind spots.

PEDIGREE GIRLS

Is this scarf yours?

Nope. I found it on this chair.

I like it.

But it's not yours.

It could be.

PEDIGREE GIRLS

What do you *mean,* you're not coming to my house after school?

I have a job interview.

Wanna come? They said they were looking to hire a lot of people.

A job? Well, I'm *rich,* in case you haven't noticed.

PEDIGREE GIRLS

You know, it's not going to work out.

Being lovers and roomies has really taken a toll on our friendship. Actually, I'm sick of you.

Oh, and I had *so* enjoyed flossing my teeth with your pubic hair.

PEDIGREE GIRLS

You know Kelly Barthes?

You mean, "Smelly Fart?"

Oh, that's *real* mature.

PEDIGREE GIRLS

My brother tells me that every morning during roll call, the whole class erupts in laughter.

The twins are in his homeroom: Andrew and Peter Ness.

A. Ness and P. Ness?

PEDIGREE GIRLS

Your dad's a great guy.

Yeah, he's pretty cool.

I just wish sometimes he'd be more demonstrative with his love.

Well, he's never had a problem doing that with *me*.

PEDIGREE GIRLS

Yeah, I'm working at the U.N. this summer.

That's a *nice* job. How'd you swing that?

Oh, you know. My dad pulled a few strings.

The only string I've got to pull is the one on my tampon.

PEDIGREE GIRLS

God, Mr. Stephens was *sooo* funny this morning. My cheeks hurt from smiling so much.

I know. I thought your face would *freeze* that way.

PEDIGREE GIRLS

God, I'm such a nerd.

No you're not.

Well, okay. Yes you are.

PEDIGREE GIRLS

The good thing about AIDS is that whoever gives it to you dies too.

That's a comfort.

PEDIGREE GIRLS

I've never been intimate with a *girl* before.

This is *fun!*

And it'll be even *more* fun once we get our clothes off!

PEDIGREE GIRLS

Who's that?

He's my bodyguard.

Dad laid off 1,200 workers and he's worried about kidnappers.

Wow!

Isn't he cute behind those dark glasses?

Maybe you can get him to do some after-hours "under-covers" work.

PEDIGREE GIRLS

How come there are always "Missing" posters but never any "Found" ones? I mean, I'd like to hear some good news for a change.

The way it is now, you get the impression kids just go missing and they're never found. They simply vanish.

PEDIGREE GIRLS

Rabid kids go for the throat. Hard-edged fatalism. Commercialized, co-opted profit-prophets. Drugged-up excess. Fin-de-siècle uneasiness. Narcoticized nerve...

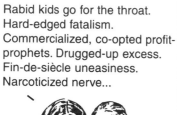

...Extremist vibes. Been there, done that, watched it all fail. Milked my once pert tits flat.

Excuse me while I go commit suicide.

PEDIGREE GIRLS

I hate parties.

You have to entertain on the most immediate level, or perish.

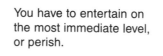

Gee, I don't know. That's my whole reason for living.

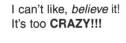

PEDIGREE GIRLS

A.　B.

C.　D.

E.　F–　OFF!

PEDIGREE GIRLS

Don't kill yourself.　Yeah. *Don't.*

You'll go to hell.　Yeah. *Hell.*

This was a very *special* episode of the "Pedigree Girls".　Yeah. *Special.*

PEDIGREE GIRLS

I'm pretty sure all the Smurfs were gay.　Like, *totally.*

Like, *"Ohhh,* how much further, Papa Smurf!"

"Oh! Not far now! Just a little deeper!"

Ha ha ha!

PEDIGREE GIRLS

Rub my nipples.

Okay.

Look. They like you.

PEDIGREE GIRLS

Look! *Tom Cruise!*

Where?!

Ha ha ha!

Bitch. You always do that.

You always fall for it.

PEDIGREE GIRLS

Emme, could you return my hair brush?

What's the magic word?

NOW!!!

God, who put the razor blades in *your* Halloween apples?

PEDIGREE GIRLS

Here's your brush back.

Thanks. I'm grateful. Now I won't have to kidnap your little sister and hold her for ransom, possibly killing her in the process.

Gimme that brush *back*.

PEDIGREE GIRLS

So, I'm having this cool pool birthday party, and if you bring me *two* gifts, I might ask the man at the gate to *possibly* let you in.

I'm the envy of all my friends.

PEDIGREE GIRLS

I just don't know *who* we'll get to bring canapés to the party.

Um, I'll do it, I guess.

Got *that* right.

PEDIGREE GIRLS

I hope you're not thinking of showing up at my pool party *uninvited*.

Uninvited?! You *told me* I could come!

I know. I lied.

PEDIGREE GIRLS

I hope the weather holds up for my pool party. It's so capricious these days: one moment it's sunny, and the next, torrents of rain.

You mean, like the way you invited then *un*invited me to your party?

God, Nat. You're so irreverent! So refreshing! You should *totally* come to my party!

PEDIGREE GIRLS

One.   Two.

Three.   Four.

Five.   Sex.

PEDIGREE GIRLS

Jenn stole the cookie from the cookie jar.

Who, me?

Yes, you.

Couldn't be.

Then who?

Satan.

PEDIGREE GIRLS

Ms. Zenia's awfully calm today.

Usually she's all panicky and stressed out.

And usually at us, too. Her two "trouble-makers".

Maybe she's finally decided to end it all and is at peace.

Should we do something?

I think the question is, have we done enough?

PEDIGREE GIRLS

You know, when I first got to this dyke school, I was lonely and afraid.

But you were very kind to me. How come you're so nice to me?

Here's a gentle hint: your dad's worth *20 million bucks*. Can you say, "connections"?

PEDIGREE GIRLS

Lend me a
quarter?

Sorry.
Can't.

C'mon.

Nope.

Your will is strong.
But I will break you.

PEDIGREE GIRLS

My sister got her first
training-bra yesterday.

She's got boobs?

Squint.

PEDIGREE GIRLS

At Havergal I've built great
friendships and developed
strong leadership skills. My
teachers and classmates
expect me to be the best...

...I can be. We all share an
enthusiasm for learning
and a respect for each
other's intelligence.

NOT.

PEDIGREE GIRLS

Shannon stole my boyfriend.

That's terrible!

And yours.

That bitch.

And I'm joining them tonight for a *ménage à quatre!*

There is, like, no God!

PEDIGREE GIRLS

It was so cool. In art class today we had this male model who was a total hottie, and we were all, like, flashing him.

And the poor guy got an erection. I mean, what do you expect? But Ms. Sawyer saw it and asked him to leave.

How did your drawing turn out?

I was inspired, so I rose to the occasion.

PEDIGREE GIRLS

Going to the father-daughter dance?

I would, but my dad's in prison.

Oh god, I'm sorry.

You *should* be...

...*you're* the one who brought charges against him!

PEDIGREE GIRLS

I'm sorry Tori, but your dad is a self-centred pig.

Well, of course he is! That's why they call them "Old Boys"...

...instead of "Old Men."

PEDIGREE GIRLS

Sarah's got six toes on her right foot.

You serious?

I saw it in gym. She's a mutant!

You're a mutant.

PEDIGREE GIRLS

Try to guess the word in my head and you can come to my cottage.

Um, tree?

Nope.

No.

You suck at this.

Secrecy?

Cadillac?

Forget it. I want out.

Keep talking.

PEDIGREE GIRLS

This is boring. Yeah.

At least we're not assholes.

PEDIGREE GIRLS

Food. Money. Sex.

Yes!

Yes!

PEDIGREE GIRLS

Lara, what can you tell me about your brother? He's sooo hot.

My brother? Hmmm. Orgasms relieve stress, not guilt.

Believe me. I've tried.

PEDIGREE GIRLS

Panel 1: That's a cute baby. — Thanks.

Panel 2: Boy or girl? — Neither. Demon spawn, in fact.

Panel 3: Oh yes— *now* I see it.

PEDIGREE GIRLS

Panel 1: People come to this strip expecting some kind of wisdom.

Panel 2: And if not wisdom, at least some sort of humour.

Panel 3: Well, they won't get it.

PEDIGREE GIRLS

Panel 1: What'd they say in chapel this morning?

Panel 2: God made men out of dust.

Panel 3: There. That *proves* men are lower than dirt.

PEDIGREE GIRLS

What are you going to be when you grow up?

A gold-digger, I guess.

You're serious?

Sure. It's easy.
Show a little leg at the right parties and see who bites.
Do the honeymoon thang, then cash in the husband. Simple. At least that's what my mom says.

PEDIGREE GIRLS

How come we're so attracted to looks? Skimpy clothes, massive endowments, glitz, glamour, and the catchy meaninglessness of it all?

Yet, the truly meaningful, the inspirational, the encouraging, wise and loving go unnoticed?

Sorry, what did you say? There was this total hottie walking by...

What? Where?

PEDIGREE GIRLS

Want some Kool-Aid?

Sure. Thanks.

Tasty.

The antidote'll be 20 bucks.

Aw, fuck.

PEDIGREE GIRLS

At one point in my life I was seeking out abusive men. I knew it was majorly unhealthy, but I couldn't help myself. But no more.

Now I'm seeking out *girls.*

Oh goody!

PEDIGREE GIRLS

You know that smile that gymnasts put on their face as they're being introduced and just before they go into their routine?

Sure.

Well, I've been practising.

You have?

How's it look?

You're radiant.

PEDIGREE GIRLS

I have to leave BSS. Dad's lost his job and my marks aren't high enough to get me a scholarship.

We'll still keep in touch and get together once in a while though, won't we?

Heather, of course. This doesn't mean that I'll ignore you, forget to return your calls and pretend you never existed. *Don't be silly!*

PEDIGREE GIRLS

That bitch, Ms. Webb. The next time I see her I hope she's under a bus.

She's right *behind* you.

Oh... heh, heh... well, that was just a figure of speech.

PEDIGREE GIRLS

Look at this: "Needed: 90 overweight people for a new advanced monitored weight reduction, nutrition, and exercise program.

Kendall really came through for us.

I hope they're tender.

Yeah, I don't want to be eating senior citizens forever.

PEDIGREE GIRLS

Do your parents still have sex?

Oh God, don't even ask...

...even the thought of Miss Piggy and Kermit the Frog *kissing* makes me shudder.

PEDIGREE GIRLS

You know, I read that the odds of being captured and killed by a serial killer are 1 in 1,450,000.

I'm feeling lucky. Why don't you go wander outside alone?

PEDIGREE GIRLS

Who's the prettiest girl of all?

You're supposed to say, "You are".

Oh, grow up.

PEDIGREE GIRLS

How come you've been drinking so much?

Sometimes I just don't want to be reminded of my life, alright?

You mean like how you envy other people's good fortune?

How you can't get a boyfriend?

Yeah.

That's enough.

How you're such a loser?

I said **shut up!**

PEDIGREE GIRLS

Who are we debating with after school? North Toronto.

Those pathetic public-school casualties.

Go for the jugular.

PEDIGREE GIRLS

I hear your parents are getting a divorce. Yeah, I'm a rope in a tug-of-war.

Why're they splitting? They're both bored.

Nice to know that "for better or for worse" still means something.

PEDIGREE GIRLS

You're an idiot.

No I'm not.

If you contradict me again, you're *not* my friend anymore.

PEDIGREE GIRLS

What happened? I saw you knee your brother in the groin. You must still be angry he sold those nudie pics of you.

Yeah, something like that.

Did you knee him so he'd apologize?

No. I kneed him *before* he could apologize.

PEDIGREE GIRLS

You're dad's hot. Is that a new moustache on him?

Yup.

I can see the family resemblance.

Shut up.

PEDIGREE GIRLS

Did you study?

As *if.*

Like, what's the point?

I know...

We're white.

PEDIGREE GIRLS

How big is the universe?

Shut up.

Is time travel possible?

Are you high?

Yes.

Okay, then.

PEDIGREE GIRLS

My mom got me two invites to the Gucci fall collection show in Milan.

Wow.

When are we going?

We're not.

You're going?

Very good. You get a gold star.

PEDIGREE GIRLS

Whatcha reading?

Never Too Thin.

Let me see?

Oh. It's *against* dieting.

PEDIGREE GIRLS

PEDIGREE GIRLS

PEDIGREE GIRLS

PEDIGREE GIRLS

Whatcha eating?

Bean burrito.

Can I have a bite?

Gnaw on your fist.

PEDIGREE GIRLS

I had such a blast last night. I got sooo drunk.

How drunk?

Like I said, sooo drunk.

But *how* drunk? What'd you do?

How am I s'posed to remember, Trish? I was drunk!

PEDIGREE GIRLS

Do you think beautiful people like themselves more?

I know *you* do.

Oh, so you're saying I'm *beautiful*?

Forget it.

PEDIGREE GIRLS

Touch it.

No.

C'mon. Where's your sense of adventure?

PEDIGREE GIRLS

I lost a sock in the laundry yesterday.

No you didn't...

I took it.

PEDIGREE GIRLS

God, your house is so big.

I always feel like I don't belong here.

Well, you *don't.*

PEDIGREE GIRLS

Seen 'Nessa lately?

Nah. She's, like, one of those people who drops everyone the second she gets a boyfriend.

That's so fucked up.

Yeah.

I wish I had a boyfriend.

Me too.

PEDIGREE GIRLS

I spoke to the guidance counsellor today.

You mean about your anti-social tendencies?

Yeah.

What'd she have to say to you?

Surprisingly, quite a lot— after I untied her.

PEDIGREE GIRLS

My brother just won the lottery!

Wow! What's he going to do with all that money?

Buy you.

PEDIGREE GIRLS

You ate my *mother*!

What have you got to *say* for yourself?

She could've used a little more salt.

PEDIGREE GIRLS

I can't believe the attitude you're copping. You think that just because my parents are rich and influential, everything gets handed to me.

But success requires hard work, determination, luck and sacrifice to succeed.

Alright, alright, I'm sorry.

Daddy had to make at least *two* phone calls to land me that job.

PEDIGREE GIRLS

Eat me out?

Only if you return the favour.

You're a tough negotiator, but I think we have a deal.

PEDIGREE GIRLS

How come there are no people in wheelchairs in comics?

Or those who talk in sign language?

Or those who use seeing-eye dogs?

Or disembodied talking heads?

Oh, wait, that's us.

Oh, right.

PEDIGREE GIRLS

Found a dress for the prom yet?

I found this coral-blue spaghetti strap number.

Weird. I've got one that sounds exactly the same.

I know.

I'll be going as you.

PEDIGREE GIRLS

I'll read you your horoscope. What's your sign?

Aries.

Uh-oh.

What?! What does it say?

"You will be hit by a bus tomorrow at 4:18 p.m."

It doesn't say that! Lemme see!

PEDIGREE GIRLS

Hey, nice skirt.

It's *your* skirt. I borrowed it from you last month.

Oh, really? Mind if I borrow it back?

Not at all...

...just don't forget to return it.

PEDIGREE GIRLS

Comics seem *sooo* benign.

Yeah. People read us like they're eating dessert.

We're taken in without criticism, without a censor.

We're the *crack cocaine* of propaganda.

KILL YOUR MOTHER.

FUCK YOUR FATHER.

PEDIGREE GIRLS

I am so fucking *horny!*

Me too.

PEDIGREE GIRLS

What's so goddamned funny?

You.

Stop laughing. I'm not funny.

Stop it.

PEDIGREE GIRLS

Bonjour classe!

Bonjour Madame!

Classe, quelle est la date aujourd-hui?

The day you die, witch.

Ha ha ha!

PEDIGREE GIRLS

God, I hate Amber. She wouldn't be so powerful without her posse.

I mean, it's no secret that they want you to kill yourself.

Well, here's my plan: I'll live up to their expectations.

That'll learn 'em.

It's settled, then. I'll hang myself.

Hey, listen, I've got this *great* outfit to be found in.

PEDIGREE GIRLS

PEDIGREE GIRLS

PEDIGREE GIRLS

PEDIGREE GILS

PEDIGREE GIRLS

So how was your date?

We drove out to the airport to watch the planes take off. The smog enveloped us and by the end, I was puking on the pavement, with him holding my hand.

I loved every minute of it!

PEDIGREE GIRLS

I've always liked Eddie Haskell.

I've always liked Wally.

Figures.

What's *that* supposed to mean?

You're a "Wally" type.

And you're a *bitch*.

PEDIGREE GIRLS

This comic strip isn't going anywhere.

What makes you say that?

PEDIGREE GIRLS

PEDIGREE GIRLS

PEDIGREE GIRLS

PEDIGREE GIRLS

Sign my yearbook?

\

Anything.

Sure. What should I write?

/

Hey. You know what I mean.

\

PEDIGREE GIRLS

Get rid of those socks. They're sooo ugly.

\

Hey.

/

Don't be like that to me.

/

Love me.

/

PEDIGREE GIRLS

How come you're so mean to me?

\

I'm insane.

/

You are *not.*

\

Roast.

/

What?

\

Cabinet.

/

PEDIGREE GIRLS

You're a pale imitation of reality.

Why?

You've got no arms, torso or legs.

They're out of the frame.

What frame?

Can a fish see the water it's swimming in?

PEDIGREE GIRLS

I can't believe we were tied up and robbed .

How do we get out of here?

Well, let's try to loosen these ropes. Is that your hand?

Yeah.

It's warm.

PEDIGREE GIRLS

What's it like to be you?

What do you mean?

I mean, to be as popular as you are.

I always thought that if I were popular that my life would be different.

Well, it's nice, I guess. People pay attention.

Do you get more guys?

More than *you.*

PEDIGREE GIRLS

I'm sleepy.

Want to come to my room for a nap?

No funny business?

None. I promise.

But, why not?

PEDIGREE GIRLS

Knock knock.

Who's there?

Who's there?

It's me.

Oh, hi.

PEDIGREE GIRLS

God, I'm happy.

You look it. What's up?

Ben licked me for *hours* last night.

That's great! Did you have sex?

Have you lost your *mind?* Have sex with my *dog?*

Oh, sorry.

PEDIGREE GIRLS

Where's your dad these days?

The casino.

He gambles?

He "speculates".

What?

The Toronto Stock Exchange casino.

PEDIGREE GIRLS

Are you coming over to prep for the prom tonight?

Sure.

Which one is your house again?

You know—the one all the police cars were in front of the other night.

PEDIGREE GIRLS

My dad keeps saying he's going to kill Cara and me, and then himself. You know, to punish my mom.

Oh, that's awful!

By the way, could I get my sweater back from you?

PEDIGREE GIRLS

PEDIGREE GIRLS

PEDIGREE GIRLS

PEDIGREE GIRLS

Those pretty girls think they're so fucking special.

Hold on, just because someone's pretty doesn't always mean they feel good about themselves.

Who asked *you*?

PEDIGREE GIRLS

The iced caffe lattes in this place are amazing!

Oh, yeah. I totally agree with you.

You'd *better*.

PEDIGREE GIRLS

Omigod!

What is it?

I just saw Angie get pulled into a car by two men! I'm worried!

Don't worry. I'm sure the kidnappers can take care of themselves.

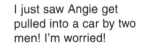

PEDIGREE GIRLS

PEDIGREE GIRLS

PEDIGREE GIRLS

PEDIGREE GIRLS

I'm hungry.

What are you thinking of?

You.

Listen, if you eat me I'll make you *fat*.

You? You're a *snack*.

PEDIGREE GIRLS

What happened to you?

What do you mean?

You used to be a tomboy. We used to be *wild*. We used to have *fun*.

What do you mean? We can still have fun being shy, obedient, quiet and pretty.

PEDIGREE GIRLS

People can be so cruel.

I know what you mean.

No you don't, you *fat fuck*.

What?!

Now you know what I mean.

PEDIGREE GIRLS

I was lifeguarding at the beach today.

And?

And these kids were waving to me from the deep waters.

Did you wave back?

Yeah, but they disappeared before they saw me.

How rude.

PEDIGREE GIRLS

I still can't believe you hired someone to kill me just because I didn't invite you to my cottage.

Well, fuck...

...I said I was sorry.

PEDIGREE GIRLS

You're pregnant? Who's the father?

It's God's child.

Alright, don't tell me. Smile your Mona Lisa smile.

PEDIGREE GIRLS

Is that a bruise?

Um, no.

PEDIGREE GIRLS

If that's a bruise, you should get some help.

It's not a bruise. It's a *subdermal contusion*.

Well, that's different, then.

See? Nothing to get excited about.

PEDIGREE GIRLS

So, I was cutting myself with a razor last night in the living room, and my mom walks in on me.

Boy, she must have freaked.

Yeah. She was like, *"Don't you dare get blood all over my new couch!"*

PEDIGREE GIRLS

Shit. You're cutting yourself *again*?

No worries. It's under stuff, so no one will see the scars.

Why do you do it?

It relieves stress.

You *might* try smoking.

Are you kidding? Smoking'll *kill* you.

PEDIGREE GIRLS

You're not alone.

I am sooo proud of you. I think you're *amazing.* I love you.

Cue the piano music.

PEDIGREE GIRLS

I need to write a suicide note.

Omigod! You're killing yourself?

Yeah. So, like, write it, then put my name on it, willya?

You mean, like I do for your homework?

PEDIGREE GIRLS

I'm in love with Edie.

You mean in grade 12?

I just want to lick her from head to toe.

How uncivilized.

This from a girl who sneaks peeks at my bum during gym.

Not just *your* bum.

PEDIGREE GIRLS

I found orange Tang crystals in my pubic hair this morning.

Oh, really?

Let me see what colour your tongue is.

PEDIGREE GIRLS

So, I'm working at Holt's and this lady walks in with an enormous Armani handbag, reeking to high heaven of Chanel No. 5, and yelling incoherently at us.

She abuses us and we have to take it because she usually drops at least a grand on clothes. Sometimes they close the store and models pose in the clothes for her.

We have those at our store, too. We call 'em stinky *bag* ladies.

PEDIGREE GIRLS

God. The only reason that guy is sooo good looking is to pop a lot of cherries...

...including mine, which I really *resent.*

PEDIGREE GIRLS

Want to do each other's hair tonight?

Sure.

Afterwards we can murder my mother.

Um, pass.

You're no fun.

PEDIGREE GIRLS

I mean, falling for your best friend, especially if it's a girl, is *traumatic...*

I mean... you know...

...so I've heard.

PEDIGREE GIRLS

Omigod! Felicia! You never told me my blind date would be with *you*!

Oh.

So, I see that no introduction is necessary.

PEDIGREE GIRLS

Ohhh, I like him.

Devon?

Yeah.

But he's Asian.

So what?

Look, tan and beige clash.

PEDIGREE GIRLS

God, we're really good friends, aren't we? I mean, I'd even say you're my *best* friend.

Sure.

PEDIGREE GIRLS

I hate abortion clinics. They're full of people not smart enough not to make more versions of themselves.

Hey! Why d'ya think I asked you here? *I'm* pregnant.

Like I said...

PEDIGREE GIRLS

Alex dumped me.

Oh, that's terrible! I feel so much sympathy for you.

It'll pass.

PEDIGREE GIRLS

Omigod! Not again!

What is it?

Puberty is sending me through panties like kleenex.

PEDIGREE GIRLS

Sure, you can come over for dinner. Meeting my girl-friends always causes my daddy's ulcer to bleed.

Finally. Thank you.

No, thank *you*.

PEDIGREE GIRLS

So you want to go for a coffee?

Let's fuck.

What?!

Some of us are falling *asleep* here.

PEDIGREE GIRLS

I can't believe they're shooting a film here!

Another affluent prep school flick full of sex, drugs and...

...an unknown serial killer!

When does it begin?

As soon as I can lure the star into the boiler room.

PEDIGREE GIRLS

So, I just signed over my dead parents' fortune to you...

...but what are you going to do with it? I don't understand.

I was counting on that.

PEDIGREE GIRLS

So, how
do I look?

You know those
supermodels?

Omigod!
Yes.

Well, you
look nothing
like them.

PEDIGREE GIRLS

When I was 13 I swore
never to take drugs
because I thought, what
if I become president?

But I got
over *that.*

PEDIGREE GIRLS

So, I switched from using
#36 Golden Tresses to
using #42 Barbie
Blonde...

...but my boyfriend
didn't even notice!

Talk about
missing the
obvious.

PEDIGREE GIRLS

You know that sexist pig that was hiring?

And I told you to tailor yourself for the job?

Right. Well, it worked! I got the job.

Great!

Now I can take these tissues out of my bra.

PEDIGREE GIRLS

Omigod! Like, when I went to the bathroom this morning, there were all these little white things crawling around my pubic hair.

Talk about a *bad hair day!*

PEDIGREE GIRLS

So how's your mom doing?

She's investing with a 20 percent return!

That's nothing! My mom's getting a 50 percent return!

That's incredible! But how?

Divorce.

PEDIGREE GIRLS

So, this is it. The comic strip.

Yup.

I don't get it. What's the punchline? Where's the joke?

You're the joke.

PEDIGREE GIRLS

I'm a little concerned about your barely suppressed anger.

Jean, don't worry. I'm more likely to kill myself than kill someone else.

What a relief!

PEDIGREE GIRLS

You're serious?

Dead.

How?

With your dad's gun.

Pardon me? I didn't catch that.

Oh, alright. With your dad's gun, *please.*

PEDIGREE GIRLS

So, how are you doing?

I'm going to throw myself off a bridge!

Um, maybe you should talk to a guidance counsellor about that.

She's the one that suggested it!

PEDIGREE GIRLS

Let's get off this ledge, okay?

Okay.

That's *not* what I meant.

PEDIGREE GIRLS

So, what's this big secret you were going to tell me?

My dad's in prison.

Really? So you were lying to me this *whole* time!

Wait a minute. I wasn't lying...

...I told you he was living in a *gated community!*

PEDIGREE GIRLS

Let's play.

Okay.

I'm a shark.

What'll I be?

Bait.

PEDIGREE GIRLS

Kris, you're so sexy, I could just eat you up.

I'm not Kris. I'm her twin sister, Kira.

Well, that goes for you too.

PEDIGREE GIRLS

I want a rich boyfriend.

That's sooo superficial!

Personally, I don't care if a boy has a lot of money...

...as long as his family does.

PEDIGREE GIRLS

I think I might be pregnant. I don't know what to do.

Liz, Liz, Liz...

...no one wants to hear it.

PEDIGREE GIRLS

I think having a beauty contest is a great idea!

Ironic considering our school's feminist mandate.

That's it, exactly!

I love that we're the judges.

Popularity, at last!

PEDIGREE GIRLS

What should the Miss Branksome Pageant posters say?

That hot guys will be ushers.

Wow. Really?

No. But see how it got your attention?

PEDIGREE GIRLS

I fucked your boyfriend last night.

Hey...

...that's mine.

PEDIGREE GIRLS

I think our uniforms have definitely become sexualized.

And fashionable. I don't like being part of a trend.

We are distorted, commercialized and offered up for consumption.

Kilts are being divorced from their *true* meaning.

What *does* a kilt mean?

That we're sexy as hell.

PEDIGREE GIRLS

Do you really think she'll drop out?

I don't know. Keep your fingers crossed.

I mean, what was she thinking, wearing her socks up like that? Did she, like, think she was one of us or something?

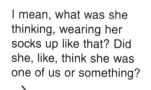

It's time to thin the herd.

PEDIGREE GIRLS

What do you want to be when you grow up?

I don't think I'll last past next spring.

I mean, why did you become a lemming?

I don't know. Everyone else did.

PEDIGREE GIRLS

My mom wants me to bring home someone she can sleep with.

You gonna?

I owe her.

PEDIGREE GIRLS

Chelsea?

What?

I've got a confession to make.

Good for you.

I have a dick.

Good for *me*.

PEDIGREE GIRLS

Okay. I know you want your dad killed. I have a friend who knows someone who can help you.

Are you out of your mind?!

How much?

PEDIGREE GIRLS

I mean, I totally can't see how Brad could have stood me up.

On purpose.

PEDIGREE GIRLS

The sad fact is that looks really are the most important thing.

Take, for example, you and me.

Okay... just take me.

PEDIGREE GIRLS

Nicole, sometimes you exaggerate things to make a point.

I know.

But sometimes you go too far. People think you're scary.

Scary? How?

Scary like fucked up, shitless scary, you know.

Don't worry. They won't be thinking a *thing* after Monday.

PEDIGREE GIRLS

PARADISE

FALL

REDEMPTION

PEDIGREE GIRLS

Going to the dance?

Sure.

Who're you taking?

Oh, nobody. Just me, myself, and I. Ha ha ha. And you?

Oh, just me and my ugly needs... ha ha ha.

PEDIGREE GIRLS

Want to play
Russian
roulette?

Sure.

I've even
got my
dad's gun.

Cool.

Well...
you first.

PEDIGREE GIRLS

God, Blair. I love that you
work here. You can get me
deals, can't you? Say, do
you have these pumps in
a size eight?

Well, we've
got a lot more
in the back...

...as
do you.

Shut up.

PEDIGREE GIRLS

I hear recylcing
only accounts
for 0.004% of all
landfill volume.

But it
removes
40% of
consumer
guilt.

I hear recylcing
only accounts
for 0.004% of all
landfill volume.

But it
removes
40% of
consumer
guilt.

I hear recylcing
only accounts
for 0.004% of all
landfill volume.

But it
removes
40% of
consumer
guilt.

PEDIGREE GIRLS

So, I had this awesome dream last night.

Oh yeah?

Yup. I dreamed that—

Don't *tell* me!

Why not?

You'll spoil it for me.

PEDIGREE GIRLS

I know it was you.

Me? What?

Who wrote, *"Kill yourself. Yours truly, God"* in my diary.

Well, *obviously* it wasn't from *me*.

PEDIGREE GIRLS

Don't lie.

I'm not lying.

Admit it, you vandalized my diary!

Well, you left it in plain sight underneath your mattress for *anyone* to find!

PEDIGREE GIRLS

PEDIGREE GIRLS

PEDIGREE GIRLS

PEDIGREE GIRLS

I mean, I've been lonely all my life, and I'm not even that nice a person...

...but I'm really glad you're my friend. I'm glad we're best friends. I love you.

Like, I *totally* agree. I love me too.

PEDIGREE GIRLS

Did your dad buy you that convertible?

Get real.

Did he take you out to dinner?

Get *realer*.

Did he take you to a hotel?

Too real!

PEDIGREE GIRLS

What do you want to be when you grow up?

A paid assassin.

Jesus. You'd kill people for money?

I'd kill my dad for *free*.

PEDIGREE GIRLS

What are you getting for Christmas?

Breast reduction surgery.

Oh, no! I love your breasts.

I don't.

Why not?

They're testicles.

PEDIGREE GIRLS

We have to talk.

About what?

About the orange powdered shit you sprinkle on your vulva.

Oh, *that...*

Girls lick more when there's *flavour.*

PEDIGREE GIRLS

What do you think is the fastest way to get Jake into bed?

Force him.

I *do* have a black belt.

Hmmm...

...I would try a garter belt first!

PEDIGREE GIRLS

God! This school is sooo conservative!

I know. I mean, I thought more people would be having sex.

People *are* having sex...

...just not *you*.

PEDIGREE GIRLS

You're kind of like my sidekick, aren't you?

No.

Oh, come off it. I mean, we all would like to think we're the stars of our own lives, but you're the wisecracking, weird-looking girl who hangs out with the more popular, better-looking one.

Like I said, you're my side—**OW!**

I think the operative word here is *kick*.

PEDIGREE GIRLS

I had sex on a first date. Was I being stupid?

No more than usua— no, of course not.

PEDIGREE GIRLS

Do you ever want kids?

You mean, like buying someone's first-born child?

No. I meant, like kids of your own.

You mean, for dinner?

No, like... forget it.

Is this a trick question?

PEDIGREE GIRLS

YAWN!

"Cocksucker's cramp?"

Jealous?

PEDIGREE GIRLS

Cooo! Cooo!

Hey. There's a pigeon just outside the window.

Are you thinking what I'm thinking?

DINNER!

PEDIGREE GIRLS

PEDIGREE GIRLS

PEDIGREE GIRLS

PEDIGREE GIRLS

PEDIGREE GIRLS

PEDIGREE GIRLS

PEDIGREE GIRLS

Ready for dinner?　Sure.

Well?

The kitchen's that way. I'll be in my room.

PEDIGREE GIRLS

Stop picking that scab!　I can't help it. It's sooo itchy.

That's ridiculous! You wouldn't sleep with your brother just because you were *horny*, would you?

Would you?

PEDIGREE GIRLS

You crazy bitch, why did you kill my parents?

Because you deserve better.

Well, alright. You're not so bad.

PEDIGREE GIRLS

You've got a fat ass.

What the *fuck?!* Why did you just *say* that?!

Dee, I'm your *best friend...*

...and as your best friend, I *owe* it to you to reveal uncomfortable truths.

PEDIGREE GIRLS

Oh, Courtney, I'm sooo glad you're okay with me going out with your ex. Oh! They're playing "Dancing Queen"! I've gotta go dance! Watch my purse, will ya?

You go girl!

Bitch.

PEDIGREE GIRLS

God, I hate this school.

Why?

Well, it's sooo fucking conservative. They'll punish you if you wear a little lipstick. The smallest thing causes *huge* controversy. There are too many privileged and ignorant WASPs here.

Wait a minute... what do *insects* have to do with this?

PEDIGREE GIRLS

C'mon.
It'll be fun.

Wipe your
own bum.

PEDIGREE GIRLS

Amanda, I hate to tell you
this, but your boyfriend and I
have fallen in love with each
other. He wants to break up
with you.

Well, I don't
believe you.

I swear to God!
May you get hit by
a *bus* if I'm lying!

PEDIGREE GIRLS

Cathryn, sometimes I feel
like you're walking on
eggshells around me. You
totally don't have to. Be
yourself. Do what you want.

PEDIGREE GIRLS

What's up?   My mom's closet is full.

What's she gonna do about it?   The usual.

Move.

PEDIGREE GIRLS

My dad told me the next time I'm complaining about something to think about what the blind guy begging in the wheelchair is feeling.

Ha Ha Ha !!!

PEDIGREE GIRLS

Whenever I drink coffee I get horny.   Really? It makes me shit.

Really? Hmmm...

I think this could be the beginning of a beautiful friendship.

PEDIGREE GIRLS

Still seeing Craig?

Nope.

Single again?

Um, between boyfriends.

PEDIGREE GIRLS

I've started working at my dad's ad agency.

That's great! What's the first thing you've sold?

Myself.

PEDIGREE GIRLS

Come closer!

I can't. My arm's in the way.

Well, cut it off then.

PEDIGREE GIRLS

PEDIGREE GIRLS

PEDIGREE GIRLS

PEDIGREE GIRLS

PEDIGREE GIRLS

PEDIGREE GIRLS

PEDIGREE GIRLS

My boyfriend's been dead now for two weeks...

...and the sex just keeps getting *better and better.*

PEDIGREE GIRLS

Would you eat me if I was the last piece of meat on a desert island?

Yeah, I'm gonna eat you...

...but, why dwell?

PEDIGREE GIRLS

Where'd you get that swank bag?

My dad got it for me.

What? He didn't get *me* one?

PEDIGREE GIRLS

I'm sad.
Can I have
a hug?

What's a
hug?

Oh, come on. Didn't your
parents ever give you a
hug when you were
younger?

Oh, *that*. They didn't
want to spoil us, you
see.

PEDIGREE GIRLS

Victoria, please. Eat
something or your
anorexia will come
back. As it is you're all
skin and bones!

It's not my fault. No matter
how much I eat I can't seem
to gain any pounds!

I see you have the
opposite problem.

PEDIGREE GIRLS

Hey, when is this so-called
"boyfriend" of yours going to
materialize?

He doesn't want
to meet you.

I'm sooo offended!
How can someone in your
head hold so much
resentment against someone
he's never even met?

PEDIGREE GIRLS

PEDIGREE GIRLS

PEDIGREE GIRLS

PEDIGREE GIRLS

Wow. You broke Lauren's arm *and* stole her Lancôme make-up kit. Is it because she called you white trailer-trash only here on a charity scholarship?

Nope. Random violence.

PEDIGREE GIRLS

Why do you hate me?

You're a snob.

Jesus H. Christ! I just got here *yesterday!*

Name-dropping *already?*

PEDIGREE GIRLS

Where's your sister, Mich?

I ate her.

Oh. Are your parents going to have another?

No. They're trying to teach me a lesson...

...if you eat your siblings, you're going to be *alone.*

PEDIGREE GIRLS

Omigod. The world's changing so *fast* these days, isn't it Liz?

Liz isn't here right now.

PEDIGREE GIRLS

I hate chopping onions.

Why?

It makes me cry.

Try closing your eyes.

PEDIGREE GIRLS

I mean, what's the big deal about Hitler?

He thought that white people were the best people in the whole wide world.

Sounds good to me.

PEDIGREE GIRLS

I mean, *something* had to be done.

But with a *chainsaw*?

The chainsaw was the quickest way to get things done.

But I mean, *why* did you do it?

I need rationale.

PEDIGREE GIRLS

Lend me $100?

No.

Okay, then, *give* me $100.

You're *crazy!*

Listen, we've got to work as a *team* here.

PEDIGREE GIRLS

God, it's almost six o'clock. I've gotta run.

Family dinner was never a big deal in my house.

That's cuz you *killed* your family.

PEDIGREE GIRLS

Hey, Mel, guess what?

What?

My dad just bought *your* dad's company.

And? Your point?

Give me your boyfriend.

PEDIGREE GIRLS

Um, I want a new Pentax camera for my birthday.

Katherine, I can't afford that.

Watch your mouth.

PEDIGREE GIRLS

I want to watch *Dead Poet's Society* again.

Why?

It's hard to explain, but somehow it *touched* me.

No, that was my *hand*.

Oh, right.

PEDIGREE GIRLS

Hey, Kelly, do you have any friends that *aren't* white?

Lemme see...

PEDIGREE GIRLS

You gonna?

I don't want to.

You'd fucking better.

Okay, alright.

Good. I can see that our friendship has grown.

PEDIGREE GIRLS

So, I told everyone about your genital warts.

Tara! Holy shit! I *trusted* you!

You should know better than that.

PEDIGREE GIRLS

It's hard to take the school elections seriously.

It's just a popularity contest. Every year the prettiest and richest girl wins.

Hmmm. Maybe I should run.

PEDIGREE GIRLS

God, Karen. I thought we were going to hate each other *forever.* Can you believe we were dire enemies before we became friends?

We're not friends...

...you just ceased to be a threat.

PEDIGREE GIRLS

God, these books are heavy.

That's your cue.

Oh, yeah, *right.*

PEDIGREE GIRLS

So, why did the monkey fall out of the tree? Because it was *dead!*

Ha! I *kill* me.

You're behind schedule.

PEDIGREE GIRLS

Wanna sleep with me?

Um, no.

You know, some people die without ever having slept with *anyone.*

And some people die a lot sooner because they *do.*

PEDIGREE GIRLS

What was that?

I said, okay, I'll sleep with you.

Well, I hope you're really really ready because I'm really, really good.

Afterwards we can award medals.

PEDIGREE GIRLS

How come you hate her so much?

Well, I mean, there's nothing really wrong with her, but...

...I think I can only empathize with the wounded.

Well, *that* can be arranged.

You really *are* my friend, aren't you?

PEDIGREE GIRLS

Quick! Put your hand here. The baby's kicking!

Wow! I didn't know you were pregnant.

I'm not.

PEDIGREE GIRLS

I need money.

Rob a bank.

Oh, *that's* original.

Rob *me.*

What do *you* have that *I* would want?

PEDIGREE GIRLS

Where'd Mel go? — She's gone.

She smoked up one night and the stuff triggered her hitherto latent schizophrenic tendencies. She's nuts now.

St. Clement's: Expands Minds. — Produces Vegetables.

PEDIGREE GIRLS

It's my eighteenth birthday tomorrow. — Last chance to commit a major felony.

Whatcha gonna get me? — Breakfast in bed.

Bacon and eggs? — No. A glass of piss and a plate of shit. *Of course* fucking bacon and eggs.

PEDIGREE GIRLS

Oh, Alexa, I heard. I'm sooo sorry. — No worries. It's totally okay.

I mean, I know it's not everyday your baby brother drowns in your swimming pool.

I wish.

PEDIGREE GIRLS

You want my what?! | Your first born.

You're crazy! I'm not giving you anything! | Then I'll burn your house down.

You can't be serious! | Look at me. Do I *look* like I'm joking?

PEDIGREE GIRLS

Are you going to finish that? | Are you an alcoholic or something?

Answer my fucking question.

PEDIGREE GIRLS

Okay. Here's the PIN number to my trust fund. | Thank you *sooo much!*

Your parents are tied up in the pool house. Better hurry.

Thank you *sooo much!*

PEDIGREE GIRLS

Oh, Morgan. I forgot my purse at home. Can I borrow five bucks?

No.

Then what the fuck good are you?

PEDIGREE GIRLS

I still don't understand why we have to *sacrifice* someone. I mean, what kind of school *is* this?

We have to sacrifice some- one so the crops will grow this season.

What crops? We're in the middle of a *city*.

Oh. You're right. How very perceptive of you.

Thanks. The benefits of a private-school education.

PEDIGREE GIRLS

I hate sitting at these cramped desks every day.

You become more tender the less you move.

What do you mean?

They want us tender, like veal.

You're *crazy!*

Maybe so. But *you're* lunch.

PEDIGREE GIRLS

Who do we sacrifice this month?

Courtney's been pretty uppity lately.

Do you think she'll please Ms. Webb?

Totally. Courtney's still a virgin.

I still feel totally bad about this.

You'll feel diferently, ahem, *next* month.

PEDIGREE GIRLS

How come you're so domineering?

At my center is a code, something formulated when I was so young that the reason for it is long forgotten.

Oh.

Now, don't ask any more questions!

PEDIGREE GIRLS

I watched *Thelma and Louise* again last night.

I hated it.

Two white women shooting the shit, talking about banalities.

Who on *earth* would want to see *that?*

PEDIGREE GIRLS

You've got something in your teeth.

No I don't.

Sure you do. Close your eyes and open your mouth.

Hold on. You're trying to *kiss* me again.

Don't flatter yourself. Now stop gabbing and pucker up.

PEDIGREE GIRLS

Let's go bowling.

Let's *not.*

PEDIGREE GIRLS

You've got big fingers.

You know what they say about girls with *big fingers.*

What? That they'll hit your g-spot *every* time, send you into the pleasure planet *stratosphere?*

No. Just that they're good bowlers.

PEDIGREE GIRLS

Say, Julia, could I please have my birthday party down in your family's one-lane bowling alley basement?

You know how hard it is for me to say no.

No.

PEDIGREE GIRLS

Alison, remember that night we slept together?

Of course.

Well, anyway, I had my head on your chest and... well...

What is it?

You don't have a heartbeat.

Oh, *that.*

PEDIGREE GIRLS

Omigod!

Amber, what is it?!

I lost my virginity!

That's *great!*

To a guy who probably settled for me because the girl he really liked wasn't interested.

Now, now. There's no need to be *realistic.*

PEDIGREE GIRLS

PEDIGREE GIRLS

PEDIGREE GIRLS

PEDIGREE GIRLS

So you'll let me? | Let you what?

Have your boyfriend for the weekend?

My Spidey-sense is tingling about that one...

PEDIGREE GIRLS

I can't believe it! You *killed* my parents!

Then you seduced my brother into signing the family *fortune* over to you!

Calm down. What would Jesus do?

PEDIGREE GIRLS

What's your new friend like?

Like you. But really pretty.

PEDIGREE GIRLS

God, that guy was sooo immature. I wonder how many guys are looking for their mothers?

I wonder how many girls are looking for their fathers?

I wonder how many fathers are looking for their daughters?

PEDIGREE GIRLS

I mean, what I'm saying is do you want to be my girlfriend, or do you want to be my *girlfriend?*

What?

The subtleties of my question are lost on the uninterested.

PEDIGREE GIRLS

That was a *great* movie!

Totally amazing!

Yeah, well, I guess I should be getting home.

Well, I won't keep you then.

Wait. I want to be kept.

PEDIGREE GIRLS

PEDIGREE GIRLS

PEDIGREE GIRLS

INDEX

FOR ALL YOUR LOVE, ENCOURAGEMENT & SUPPORT, THANK YOU: my parents boen-min t and judy t, and my brother sean t. You have been my beloved security blanket and best case scenario. • My heartfelt gratitude for having the chutzpah to bring this twisted vision to fruition: mike o'c, richard a, and jan b at insomniac p. You are the ones we've been waiting for. •To my co-conspirators and fellow "beautiful liars": rYAN k, margaux wullumson, angela d, becky b, mark b, "old boy irregular" and magnanimous patron to the unconscious arts james fitz, amy b, gillian w, sheridan s, jenny l, jim m, julia c, paul q, melissa k, sarah r-s, thanks to paul v for your early encouragement, editing, support and exquisite IV league emceeing, alisha b, grace l and bubble tea, caleb c, kristen p, sam l, jason k, jeff t, george b, karen h, shelley m, sarah k, yvette p & ITP, ana r & tony s, joshua l, pam w, ian r, tracie g, jim c, phil b, craig s, pat l, kim m in k-town, nath g-m, adrienne w, anne-marie p, erin o'h, marc p, dera n, emily p-w, selena l, yechel g, peter @ blizzarts, carolyn s, ciara p, emily u, dana h, thoth h, terry d, sylvat a, katherine f, matt f, lynn c, michael h, jessica m, john b, matthew v e, andy w, gina h, ron c, krista s, natasha b, maureen k, patrick v, alexis o'h, ian s, sarah r, allan b, jennifer lg, shelagh r-l, julie v for your kind comments at the MEG show, gene s @ HVW8, annika g, david o'c, lani m & stephen h. I owe you all everything. • To lindsay a, lesley a, and kait a & the rest of the A clan. You folks have been amazing. You still astound me. • To mary h and stu, chris h and cindy c, and the rest of the expanding Hunter family. Thank you for your unflagging support when all this was a tiny insane seed. Thank you for taking home Jesus, His Vogue model angels, one of the graduating classes, and the blurry Old Boys. I know they have good homes. • To john & lorraine, & sarah & caitlin d. Your lives are a light. Thank you for conversation, dinners, feedback and support during my misspent youth. • To Mrs. Talwar. For support, friendship and tea. • To the girls at Navarino's, and peter & steve, thank you for the daily touchstones of coffee, conversation, and care. • Thanks to the McGill D crew, who took this hungry wolf back in the fold, and who kept me in stitches, bandwidth, videogames, and a hangout in the months leading to hibernation. • To dj and the red h. • To the lovely groundfloor by-the-bootstrappers at SUM magazine • To dan s and becky s, who showed me how lovely christmas in connecticut could be, and how warm and lovely november could be. • To lindsay, my klepto-anarcho branksome 'mole'. Thank you for the yearbook, the tie and the pin. First, we take Toronto, then we take Berlin. • To my sometimes patron and irascible Old Boy, herb b. You know what? You're a dirty old man. But it takes one to know one, I guess. • Thanks to keith orkusz for letting me use his hauntingly luminous digital painting for my cover. • Thanks again to rYAN kAMSTRA for his punchy press releases & kick-ass back cover blurbs. • To the far-sighted insouciance of sWELL magazine. • To my long-lost penpal nadine v z, thank you for your honesty and inability to choose from an excessive selection of boots. • To donald b k, who urges me to life & health & happiness. • To julie c, for that much needed lift that day. Thank you. • To justin w: ain't life interesting? • To my cool cats and fellow felines who still sniff the 'nip: sully, joe, jing-xi, newborn "little one" margaux and missing-in-kingston mosa, and all the other unknown alley elements who paw at my window. • To those kind folks who forgave my early bungled strip. Thank you for not burying me. • Also thanks to those who helped in this strip's creation, but who would now disavow any knowledge of my actions. In case I am caught or killed, I wish you nothing but peace and prosperity for the rest of your days. • To my alma mater, queen's u, where I discovered for the first time that private schools existed, and where all of this began. • To all the more immediate angels, aswell as the undercover ones: my sincerest lifelong gratitude. • And to isabelle m, my snuggly love, for gentle times: thank you.

Sherwin Tjia is a Toronto-based painter, poet and journalist. He is pursuing a masters in fine art at Concordia University. His poetry and prose can be found in *Adbusters, dig, Quarry,Queen Street Quarterly,* and *UltraViolet*. His poetry appears in *The I.V. Lounge Reader* (Insomniac, 2001) and his first collection of poetry, *Gentle Fictions*, will be released in fall 2001.